By the same author

Billy and Me
You're the One that I Want
Dream A Little Dream

Dream A Little Christmas Dream

GIOVANNA FLETCHER

PENGUIN BOOKS

PENGUIN BOOKS

UK | USA | Canada | Ireland | Australia
India | New Zealand | South Africa

Penguin Books is part of the Penguin Random House group of companies
whose addresses can be found at global.penguinrandomhouse.com

First published 2015
001

Copyright © Giovanna Fletcher, 2015

The moral right of the author has been asserted

Set in 12/14 pt Garamond MT Std
Typeset by Jouve (UK), Milton Keynes
Printed in Great Britain by Clays Ltd, St Ives plc

A CIP catalogue record for this book is available from the British Library

ISBN: 978–1–405–92587–7

www.greenpenguin.co.uk

Dream A Little
Christmas Dream

I.

I'm warm, fuzzy and happy – deliriously high on the mulled wine we've been consuming while erecting our mammoth Christmas tree that's standing smack bang in the middle of our lounge.

One by one, Brett and I take delicate glass decorations from a dusty cardboard box on the floor and place them lovingly on to the tree; all the while giving each other smug little smiles, because we've found someone to love us during what is surely the loneliest time of year for single people. Yes, I've been there – choking on my dry roast turkey, hearing how ecstatically happy everyone else in the universe is while I'm a heartbroken and lugubrious singleton . . .

But this time it's us.

We're the joyous ones . . .

And we deserve to be just a little smug.

I grab my 'homemade' mince pies (as if I made them – I always get mine from Tesco, change the cases and then bash them up a bit to make them look more rustic), remove one from the tin and sit elegantly on Brett's knee before placing it in his gob.

He reaches over me, almost knocking me off my perch, and snatches another of my culinary delights from beside us and shoves it in my mouth – watching me closely as I bite into it.

We munch on them enthusiastically while making noises to

exclaim just how good they are (proof I definitely didn't cook them).

'Delicious,' I say gaily, puffing some of the pastry out into the air as I say it.

'Mmmmm . . .' says Brett, unperturbed by my lack of decorum and giving me an appreciative kiss on the cheek.

With She & Him's Christmas album playing in the background, we're engulfed in a magically festive atmosphere that's on a par with some of the best love scenes in cinematic history: the sexy swan/rain scene in The Notebook, the moment Sid Quest defies every scientific law and saves the day and the girl in Halo, the elegant dance number between Danny Kaye and Vera-Ellen in White Christmas showing us exactly when the best things happen . . .

We're all those scenes and more.

It's beautiful.

We're beautiful.

Suddenly the lights dim, the music gets louder and we appear in black and white – with Brett in a penguin suit (complete with a cane) and me in a 1950s frilly cocktail dress: a swishy number with intricate black floral lace woven from its tiny high-waisted belt to just below my knee.

We're on our feet, stood an arm's-width apart as we gently hold hands – gazing into each other's eyes lovingly.

As the music swells, our bodies react, pulling us closer into a classic ballroom hold. Moving like two iconic film noir superstars, we chassé and glide around the room – twirling around the newly decorated Christmas tree like professionals.

We're the image of happiness.

As I spin faster and faster, I feel something grip hold of my *foot. A quick glance tells me I've got tangled with a loop of fairy lights.*

'Not to worry,' I think to myself, gently trying to flick it off. 'This is all so festive, wonderful and enchanting — I can't stop now.'

Instead of stopping, I continue. I push off the ground with the opposite foot, snatch it up under my knee and deliver what is (without question) The Best Bloody Pirouette Ever Pirouetted.

Just as I'm rejoicing with the elation of the movement and basking in the look of wonderment on Brett's face, I feel the lead around my standing ankle tighten, then tug.

It pulls the ground from under me and sends me flying forward towards the ground.

My body can't react quickly enough. Instead of helping, my arms stay down by my sides — meaning the first thing to have contact with the ground is my jaw. It crashes into it with a crack and a grinding crunch.

Ouch.

The last thing I see are my shattered teeth flying from my mouth, through the air and on to the living room floor.

I black out as Brett looks at me in horror.

Gasping in shock, my body jolts forward. My hands fly to my mouth, protectively cupping my jaw, relieved to find a full set of gnashers still in there.

I breathe out and try to steady the adrenaline that the dream has unnecessarily sent pumping through my veins, which, in turn, has caused a flush of anxiety to niggle uncomfortably at my insides.

A warm hand from the darkness is firmly placed on my back.

'What was it this time?' Brett asks, his voice gravelly and hoarse in his slumbersome state.

Thankfully he seems to like the fact that my mind goes into overdrive during my sleeping hours, taking me to all sorts of faraway places and into the quirkiest of situations. Although little does he know that just before he came back into my life (we knew each other vaguely many moons ago), I'd been having recurring dreams of him and me together (he was my dream lover – literally – in one memorable dream we had the most explosive space sex ever). Then, just hours later, he re-entered my life and beat me to the promotion I wanted at work – it was a confusing time and utterly embarrassing. Needless to say, I never divulged any of the pre-Real Brett dreams to him. I didn't think it would be entirely appropriate to share my stalkerish dreamland tendencies and I didn't want him questioning my sanity. Luckily for me, Real Brett became even more dreamy, charismatic and funny than Dream Brett ever was – putting me in a rather happy little bubble and banishing Dream Brett altogether. Now it's all about Real Brett.

'I knocked all my teeth out,' I mumble through my hands, remembering the vision of them all spilling out.

'Come here,' he growls lovingly, pulling me down sleepily and cocooning me with his body as he throws one of his heavy legs over mine. 'We'll have to look that one up in the morning.'

I'm never too fussed about what dream books say about dreams – I mean, I know dreams have meanings, but I don't think it's as simple as one image is equal to one meaning. I think it's more complex. However, Brett loves rummaging around on Google and deciphering the madness. My madness. I get regular texts with possible meanings of my nightly escapades. It's utterly adorable that he bothers.

'It was horrible,' I grumble.

'Oh, Sarah . . .' he says softly, squeezing me into him a little bit tighter and kissing the top of my bare shoulder before flopping his head back on to his pillow. 'Sleep now. I'm here.'

Within seconds, he's lightly snoring in my ear – effortlessly back to being fast asleep.

I try to breathe him in and enjoy the warmth and comfort of having my wonderful boyfriend's arms around me in my bed. I attempt to focus on just the romantic side of my dream and how lovely, cosy and complete I felt in our festive merriment. But it's no use.

Nothing I do manages to expel the sensation of my heart leaping into my mouth as I horrifically saw myself helplessly hurtling towards the ground.

Having been woken up so violently, it's impossible to relax back into sleep.

I sigh in frustration and dramatically bash my fists against the bed, but Brett doesn't even stir.

I snarl into the dark space around me. I know it was just a dream, I know I should be able to just shrug it off and go back to sleep – but some dreams just aren't shakeable. They linger and fester, leaving you either too scared to go back to sleep, or, in the case of when I was dreaming about Dream Brett, with the biggest crush imaginable. Dreams are powerful commodities. I don't understand why everyone else can just forget them so easily.

Giving up the fight, I untangle myself from Brett's embrace, slide out from under the covers and throw on a T-shirt I find crumpled up on the floor. Now that I'm up, I need a pee.

Walking out of my room, across the hallway and into the bathroom, I switch on the light and gasp in fright.

My ditzy flatmate Carly is on the loo stark naked – well, naked apart from her lacy black knickers that have been pulled down to below her knees.

'What the fuck are you doing?' I hiss, sure I'm about to have a heart attack.

'Thank God it's you!' she whispers back, her hand on her heaving chest as she stares at me wide-eyed in shock.

'Why didn't you shut the door?' I say, closing it now.

'I didn't want to turn the lights on – it would've woken me up more,' she reasons – a logic I'd completely follow on any other given night, but we have guests. 'I didn't think anyone else was up.'

'Shitting hell,' I say, sitting on the edge of the bath as she finishes using the loo and we swap positions.

I've no problem peeing in front of my best mate – it's just something we do. It's bumping into her unexpectedly in the middle of the night in the dark that freaks me out.

'It's only five o'clock,' she says, grabbing her pink dressing gown from behind the bathroom door and covering herself up.

'Only? I thought it was the middle of the night,' I groan, running my hands along my face and stretching out the tired skin around my eyes – something I know my mum would tell me off for. 'Encouraging wrinkles, Sarah – ageing before your time . . .' Blah, blah, blah . . .

'Nope, you've slept the night away, I'm afraid. Work in a few hours . . .' Carly groans, brushing her blond hair off her face and tying it up into a messy ponytail.

'I don't think I'm going to get back to sleep now anyway,' I admit, my body still buzzing from having two huge shocks within ten minutes of each other.

'I probably won't, either,' she shrugs. There's a pause.

'*Kardashians*?' I ask, pulling up my knickers and washing my hands.

'I'll go get it ready – you grab the teas and biscuits,' she says, running off to the lounge.

Before I went and got myself a boyfriend, me and Carly were always in each other's beds, watching crap on TV while stuffing our faces with naughty treats. It was our thing, our guilty pleasure. But now that I

7

have bagged a man-friend and Carly has Josh (another of our besties – they kept us in the dark for months), we're in each other's rooms less and less. Although Brett loves Carly and Josh loves me, I think they'd object to our over-familiar ways in their presence. Plus, the bedrooms are now for 'couple time' and no one likes a third wheel. Well . . . they might, but neither of them are getting me and Carly in the sack together – sick and wrong. Just, no.

Anyway, our time together when the boys are around is generally restricted to in the lounge or general communal areas – although we still don't get to do our favourite pastime of watching crappy TV without them moaning, so we have to sneak in episodes whenever we can – like at five in the morning when we can't sleep.

Feeling like naughty schoolchildren, we sprawl out on either side of the sofa, snuggle up under the *Snowman* blanket we bought the previous weekend at a Christmas market, and start to watch the latest dramatics of Kardashian life while slurping on our teas and munching on custard creams.

We've completed one and a half episodes and have finished gnawing our way through the entire packet of biscuits when Carly presses the pause button and looks at me with a heavy sigh.

'What?' I say, eyeing her up suspiciously.

'Josh wants us to move in together.'

'What!' I squeak, sitting up.

'I know.' She nods, her green eyes shiny.

'When did he ask that?'

'Tonight, before we got into bed,' she giggles.

'Right,' I say. 'And how do you feel about it?'

'Well, we almost did before – you know . . . ' she says seriously, screwing up her nose.

'Yeah, I know,' I say, pursing my lips into a smile.

The reason Carly and Josh had to come clean about their relationship to the rest of our friendship group was because she'd fallen pregnant. Guessing that a cherub-faced little sprog would be difficult to hide, they had no choice but to tell us what had been going on. They'd talked about moving in together – had even gone as far as spending a night browsing Rightmove to see what properties were in their price range – but sadly Carly suffered an early miscarriage. It hit the pair hard, understandably, and, although they've remained together, they've never really mentioned future plans – it's been as though they've wanted to just live for today rather than plan for tomorrow. Well, until now that is.

'We never actually talked about moving after everything,' Carly muses, echoing my thoughts as she looks longingly into the empty biscuit packet. 'I think we both just wanted everything to go back to normal and forget – but now, this feels right. It's like he's asking because he genuinely wants to live with me, and not because we have a baby on the way or because he feels sad about the situation we're in.'

'A nicer way to do it all, definitely,' I say, grabbing her hand and shaking it with excitement.

Carly grins at me. 'I'm going to live with a boy!'

'That is some scary shit right there.'

'Tell me about it . . . oh, I'm going to miss you so much,' she groans, grabbing hold of my shoulders and pulling me towards her so that I'm lying next to her on the sofa. 'It's not going to change anything, though. We'll still do this,' she says, pressing the play button on the remote and cuddling me as we watch the Kardashian sisters all nibbling on salad as they have a heated family discussion about some ridiculous rumour circulating in the press. I zone out. Instead, I look around the room and imagine living here without Carly, my bestie . . . the thought makes me sad.

I've called this flat, in London's Bethnal Green, home since leaving university just shy of a decade ago. Although I'd previously lived here with my ex-boyfriend Dan (he fell out of love with me and preferred the look of Lexie – they're both in our friendship group now . . . it's fine), Carly moving in brought the place back to life, removing me from the crater of despair I was living in.

With her came the sunshine, the love, the laughter – I don't want it to go back to being just me.

And yes, I know I have Brett now and that life is a little different to the miserable lonely existence I had before Carly got back from travelling and moved in – but I don't want to pin a 'new housemate' badge on him just because my current housemate has moved out and he just happens to be about. You can't rush into these things and start thinking your relationship is somewhere that the other person might not. That's when trouble starts . . . right? Or maybe I have some deep-rooted issues, thanks to my relationship with Dan, and am now worried about talking too much about the future in case Brett doesn't think there is one?

Either way: I'm gutted Carly is going to be leaving me for love.

Stupid love. Love ruins everything . . . said no sane and happy person anywhere, ever. Bah, humbug.

2.

After a hectic day at work trying to finalise and wrap up everything before the Christmas break starts at the end of the next week, I'm walking past a parade of shops on a busy east London street when my phone vibrates in my pocket.

'Are you there yet?' I ask, once I've quickly removed a hand from its glove and jabbed at the screen several times – icy hands never seem to work well with technology.

'Yes. First one here,' says Brett.

I can imagine him sat in our regular Wednesday evening spot, eagerly awaiting the rest of us and the start of our highly competitive quiz night.

'Already got a round in for when everyone turns up,' he adds.

'Good work,' I say, imagining the warmth I'm going to be greeted with when I take that first sip of fruity, rich red wine. Yummy. 'What are you up to while you wait?'

'I've been looking up teeth falling out.'

'Oh yeah?' I groan. Having managed to finally remove the horrific image from my head I'm not overly happy to be greeted with it again.

'Yep. You're emotionally disturbed,' he says, enjoying

his declaration – I can tell he's trying not to smirk as he delivers his diagnosis.

'Tell me something I don't know.'

'Right,' he agrees. 'Apparently you're that way inclined though because you're facing some big changes in your environment.'

'Oh,' I say, thinking back to my earlier conversation with Carly – it's like my brain sensed it was about to come and gave me some warning . . . although I would rather it hadn't been delivered in such a gross and cryptic way.

'So it turns out you shouldn't have got rid of Gosling,' Brett sighs, audibly gulping on his beer.

I crack up, throwing my head back and letting out a proper belly laugh, not minding the odd looks I'm attracting from strangers walking past.

When Carly first moved into the flat, we decided to rid the place of Dan and the horrors of heartbreak, by girlifying the place. Well, what better way to do that than hanging a half-naked Ryan Gosling poster in the living room for us to marvel over at our every convenience? But last weekend, after much debate and serious consideration towards our boyfriends' feelings (it must be difficult knowing they'd never live up to the magnificence that is Ryan Gosling), we decided to remove Ryan from his perch. It was a sad, sad day . . . one that was marked with a bacon sarnie and mid-afternoon glass of wine – something had to fill the void he'd left behind.

'Maybe we should bring him back.' I smile.

Brett chortles down the line.

'No?'

'It's your flat . . .' he says, his attention suddenly elsewhere. 'Alastair and Josh have just turned up,' he explains as I hear my friends greeting him raucously in the background.

'Great – I'm just round the corner. See you in a sec,' I say, putting down the phone and saving my icicle of a hand (which I'm sure is just seconds from frostbite) in the warmth of my coat pocket.

When I get to the pub a few minutes later, Carly and Natalia have already joined the others at our usual spot in the corner.

'Drink,' Natalia says, coming at me with a glass of mulled wine and a hug.

I welcome both – squeezing her before taking a gulp.

Ah.

Warm winter heaven trickles down my throat.

'Busy day?' she asks sympathetically, her kind brown eyes furrowed in concern for my wellbeing. (Which is ironic as I know she works longer hours than the rest of us put together. Natalia never stops. Her phone is practically glued to her hand, ready for work to call with an interior design disaster – I've no doubt that even on Christmas Day she'll be on high alert, just in case the wrong shade of sofa cushion is spoiling the magical day for a wealthy client. Sounds far-fetched, but you don't know how barmy and eccentric some upper-class folk can be.)

'Normal Christmas chaos,' I admit, giving her another squeeze and finding myself envious of how beautifully put together she always looks in her work suits. I inevitably have an element of shabbiness to me, no matter how hard I try – although I'm not as scruffy and boho as Carly, who continues to look as though she's about to hit the beach in Thailand any minute.

'Can you believe you've been there almost a year?' Natalia asks as we walk towards the table and the rest of our gathered friends.

'A year since our Sarah grew some balls and told Red Brick where they could shove it.' Alastair, my man-bunned and tattooed friend grins, joining in the conversation as he affectionately shakes my shoulder.

'Thanks, guys,' I say, rolling my eyes as I remove my multiple layers of winter clothes. 'I think you'll find I've always had balls – I just used them in a very different way.'

'True story,' agrees Josh as he engulfs me in one of his magnificent hugs. Even though he's now dating Carly, I'm still graced with this simple joy. I have to admit that I'm more than glad their relationship hasn't stopped him delving out those bad boys . . . they really are hugs on another level and I don't think I could emotionally cope with life if they were ripped from it. Although it's a shame those hugs are stealing my best friend out of our flat . . .

Not that I can blame her.

Argh.

Having toured the group, I eventually get to my spot next to Brett and collapse into his arms, giving him a fantastically great smacker on the mouth.

'Your lips are cold,' he murmurs, kissing me again.

'Need warming up.' I nod with the sauciest look I can muster – a slight raise of an eyebrow and quick pout of the lips.

'Get a room!' Dan grins as he and Lexie sidle up to the table.

'Hi, guys,' smiles Lexie, looking warm and radiant.

I used to only be able to refer to Dan as my ex and Lexie as the perfect girl he left me for, but over the last year I've managed to somehow let go of all the anguish and heartache that was following me around and accept this weird group dynamic. It was understandably hard for Brett to get his head around it too, but he quickly realised I wasn't hankering to have Dan back in my life romantically and he even chivalrously escorted me to their wedding.

Thank goodness.

I mean, I'm over it and thankfully felt nothing as I saw Dan stood at the altar, but let's face it – no one wants to go to an ex's wedding . . . especially not alone, looking like some desperado still clinging on to the hope of reconciliation.

With Brett by my side, I luckily diverted that assumption from other guests – and I thanked him for being there for me by making him my boyfriend that night.

I know.

I'm so kind.

'Guys,' says Ian, the balding pub landlord and overseer of all things pub-quiz related. He's usually upbeat and excited about the quiz ahead, but tonight he seems a tad forlorn and miserable. 'Glad you're all here. I've got a bit of a problem . . .'

'What's up, big man?' asks Alastair, lounging back with his arm draped over the back of Natalia's chair – I've never thought of such a stance as suggestive in our group, but seeing as Carly and Josh were always touchy-feely and we thought nothing of it, you never can tell. Perhaps in a few months' time we'll find out these two have been bonking like rabbits too. Stranger things have happened.

'Everything still on for tonight?' Josh asks. He might be our cuddly bear, but that doesn't mean he's not the most competitive one of us all.

'What?' asks Ian, looking confused. 'Oh, yes, yes – everything's fine for tonight.'

'Thank fuck,' grins Dan, grabbing his beer and downing half of it in one.

'It's next week I have a slight problem with . . .' Ian mumbles.

'What?' squeaks Josh, the fear already present in his voice, even though he's got no idea what Ian is going to say.

The following Wednesday night quiz is the final one of the year – the one that'll decide whether we spend our Christmases as victors or losers. Needless to say, it's an important one and carries great significance.

'Well, I can't be here,' says Ian, glancing round at

the bar and looking like he'd rather be anywhere else than standing at this table giving us this quivering confession.

'What?' stammers Josh, his face losing some of its colour.

'Shit,' mutters Alastair, looking around at the rest of us who are equally as bummed out over the news.

'Oh no, why?' asks Natalia softly, sensing how awkward Ian looks and thankfully being a bit more delicate in her approach to the situation.

'Anything wrong?' I grimace.

'Family thing,' he replies, shaking his head sadly. 'A problem I need to sort.'

'Right,' says Dan, raising an eyebrow at Brett.

'Are you going to cancel the quiz, then?' asks Carly, putting a hand on Josh's leg to keep him stable in case the answer is a regrettable yes.

'Hopefully not.' Ian sighs – a sound that is echoed around our table. 'That's why I wanted to talk to you guys. I know you all love the quiz – you're here most weeks without fail. Well, I wondered if anyone would mind stepping in as quizmaster.'

'Can't one of the staff do it?' asks Alastair, looking past Ian to Becky the barmaid, who's pulling a pint of bitter for one of the locals.

'It's Christmas. Our busiest time.' Ian shrugs.

'Don't you have any friends you could ask?' asks Natalia, almost pleading.

'Sadly not. All busy. I've tried. Christmas parties to go to, presents to buy, family to see . . . you know.'

'I'll do it,' offers Brett, raising his hands up as though sacrificing himself.

'You will?' asks Ian, his face lighting up.

'Hold on a minute,' says Josh, leaning over to Brett. 'You're our best player.'

'Oi,' says Carly, pretending to be offended. 'I answer at least two questions correctly every week. Three if I'm on a roll. And Sarah's not too bad herself.'

'True, you two really do bring something special to our efforts, but, having said that, I'd much rather one of you girls took over on the mic than Brett.'

'You cheeky fucker,' laughs Carly, slapping him on the thigh.

'We play to win,' says Alastair to Brett, looking equally as unimpressed.

'Well, if no one agrees to do it, there'll be nothing to win,' Ian says regretfully.

'It's not going to come to that,' sighs Brett, frowning at the group. 'Guys, you're the originals. You started the year as just the seven of you and you should end it like that. *A* quiz is better than *no* quiz, right?'

'You're right,' caves in Josh with a sigh, looking really downtrodden. 'You girls just need to up your general knowledge by next week.'

'We'll revise non-stop,' I joke with a roll of my eyes.

Although I love the feeling of winning, the real reason I love our Wednesday nights is because it gives us an excuse to all be together – something I don't think every friendship group experiences when they leave their uni days behind them. Most disperse across the country and see each other once a month, if they're lucky – especially after so many years have drifted by.

'That's sorted then. Don't worry, Ian,' says Brett with a pensive smile as he gives him a friendly slap on the back. 'We've got this under control.'

'Thank you!' gushes Ian with a relieved grin on his face, happy to have the matter sorted. 'Free drinks all round for the inconvenience?'

'Wouldn't say no,' grins Alastair as the whole table instantly perks up.

'No drink like a free drink,' nods Dan, tilting his empty glass in Ian's direction.

Once the dust has settled over the absence of Brett on our team the following week, talk turns to normal life and Christmas plans.

'Actually, we've got some news,' says Josh, grinning at Carly.

'We've moving in together!' squeals Carly in response, doing a little jig in her chair and appearing even more thrilled about the matter than she did she when she told me earlier.

'When?' asks Natalia with a huge grin on her face – looking totally ecstatic.

'As soon as we find a place,' Josh says excitedly, pulling Carly into him.

'That's brilliant,' smiles Lexie, leaning over and placing her hand over Carly's and giving it a little rub.

'Did you know?' Brett whispers quietly into my ear.

'She told me this morning. Forgot to tell you . . .' I mumble back.

'You OK?'

'Yeah,' I say, looking up at him with a small smile that tells him that although I'm far from thrilled that my bestie is moving out of our cosy little flat, I'm pleased for her and Josh to be starting this new adventure together.

Brett puts his arm around me and holds me close. I lean into him and watch happily as our friends coo over their news.

'Actually, we've got something to share too . . .' says Lexie, tears springing to her eyes as she side glances at Dan.

He gives her an encouraging nod and shuffles in his seat.

'I'm pregnant,' she squeaks, holding her hands either side of her face and giving them a little wave of elation.

'No way!' beams Alastair, getting to his feet.

'Almost twelve weeks,' grins Dan, rubbing her non-existent bump.

'This is so exciting,' wails Natalia, tears streaming down her face instantly at the overload of information she's just received.

'Amazing news,' I chip in, aware that Brett's hold around me has stiffened.

I place my hand on his and give it a little reassuring

squeeze, signalling I'm fine with this news. It's hardly unexpected – they've been married for ten months and live in their own home. They're ready to start bringing children into their idyllic little set-up.

The thought of there being a baby in the group makes me think of Carly and what she must be feeling having lost her own just a year ago – imagining the news to stir up a mixture of emotion and sorrow. However, whatever significance I try to pin onto the situation, she appears to be nothing but happy as she dives around the table to give Lexie a hug.

I stand up and follow suit, enjoying the giddy hysteria that's settled over our table.

'Look at you all growing up,' says Natalia, wiping her eyes before picking up her wine glass and taking a gulp.

'Had to start happening at some point.' Josh shrugs, looking happier than I've ever seen him.

'Making you think about all the things we haven't got?' asks Alastair, the other remaining singleton in our group.

'Their joy brings me joy,' Natalia replies thoughtfully, raising her glass at the table and looking as though she's about to start bawling again.

'We'll get there . . . ' Alastair winks at her, giving her elbow a little nudge with his. 'And if we're both still single when we're forty –'

'Don't even go there!' she gasps, making us all laugh as she jumps away from him in disdain. 'I am not going to be a forty-year-old spinster!'

'As if you would be!' laughs Carly, squeezing hold of her tiny waist in a protective manner. 'You on the other hand . . .' she says jokily, turning to Alastair. 'A little less bed-hopping and more conversation might be the way forward.'

'What can I say?' He shrugs. 'I'm very good at forewords – there never seems to be any point in sticking around for the full novel.'

'Not yet,' said Lexie. 'But someone will come along and change that.'

'That's what everyone says,' nods Alastair. 'Seriously though, guys – stop trying to cut short my fun. I'm so chuffed for you all in your coupled merriment . . .'

'Hear, hear,' says Natalia, suddenly getting the giggles as she tops up her glass and raises it in the air. 'To the grown-ups.'

'The grown-ups,' we all chorus in salute.

'So when are you due?' Josh asks Lexie, turning the focus back onto the biggest news of the night.

'June,' she beams.

'Seems like ages away,' Dan says with a groan. 'These first few weeks have dragged so much.'

'So that's why you've not been drinking,' Carly gasps.

'You mean, there was no detox?' asks Natalia, looking equally as dumbfounded.

'A detox in December?' asks Dan, looking at us all as though we were mad to have believed his trustworthy wife.

'I knew something was up,' says Alastair with a nod, looking pleased with himself.

'No you didn't,' I laugh, picking up a crisp from the table and throwing it at him. In typical Alastair style, he effortlessly catches it in his mouth and grins back at me while munching on it.

'Pregnancy really suits you,' Carly says to Lexie. 'You're really glowing.'

'Thank you . . . I feel awful,' she says, puffing out her cheeks although unable to hide her delight at her condition.

'You're hiding it well,' Carly says kindly.

'God, I don't feel it,' Lexie giggles. 'So where are you going to move to?' she asks back.

I watch my friends (some settled and preparing for new adventures, others footloose and carefree, ready for whatever comes their way) and wonder where I fit in the whole world of 'Grown-ups'. I suddenly feel as though I'm in limbo and hate myself for the dissatisfied feeling that's beginning to slither over me . . .

3

We win. It's a landslide victory thanks to our nemesis team, the High-kick-flyers, being absent – they were off being charitable and performing Christmas carols in an old people's home nearby. So although we win by miles we know the real competition will be when they're back next week and we're not just up against the other crappy teams who seem to have a lower IQ than Joey Essex.

On the walk home, with my arm looped through Brett's, I start to ponder the icky feeling that's unexpectedly crawled up under my skin since hearing everyone's happy news. I know the feeling – it's one I've unfortunately had the pleasure of battling with before.

It's a feeling of discontent.

Of something missing.

Of knowing there's more to life than what I currently have in my lap.

The last time I had it was only a year ago – and that was largely down to my unresolved anger towards Dan and Lexie, being lonely and wanting someone to love me, having a shitty job that I was over-qualified for, and feeling like a constant disappointment to my parents (my mother in particular). Well, having let

the feeling fester for long enough, I somehow managed to eventually turn everything around. I forgave
the God-awful situation with Dan, met Brett
(although it was the dream version of Brett that actually kept me company to start with), and walked out
of my no-hope of a job into a much better one – thus
making my mum proud.

And I've still got all that.

I'm happy.

I should be happy.

So why do I suddenly feel like I'm not?

What could it possibly mean?

That I'm a greedy cow, who wants even more,
that's what. That this happy little set-up with Brett
suddenly isn't enough. It means I want more of him;
I want a future. I want to know I'm going to marry
him one day and have his babies . . . I want us to plan
to grow old and boring together.

'Where do you see us going?' I ask abruptly, without
giving my brain and heart a chance to really process
the feeling inside me that's quickly spreading through
my veins like an itchy poison. The thought of talking
about the future usually petrifies me, so God knows
why I've leapt in so carelessly without any planning or
clarity as to where I want this conversation to go.

There's a pause.

Silence.

I feel sick as I wait for a response.

'Home?' He shrugs, noncommittally, his gaze on
his size ten feet.

'And after that?' I say, nudging him slightly – both physically and mentally.

'Bed?' he asks, glancing sideways at me as though I've turned slightly crazy. 'Right?'

'Yeah.' I nod, feeling like a complete twat as I smile up at him and try desperately to blink back the tears that are stupidly threatening to spill. Seriously, what on earth is wrong with me? Though, actually, what the fuck is wrong with him?

For the last three hours we've been hearing all about Carly and Josh's hopes for their new pad and Dan and Lexie gushing as they share some baby chat – all nattering on about how great their futures are going to be. I *know* Brett knows exactly where my head is at right now, when I'm asking a question about our future, and I can't help but feel knocked back and deflated that he hasn't taken the bait and come back with something nice – even if it was just a lie.

Holy shit. What if his avoidance is because he doesn't see a future with me?

Oh fuck! Oh fuckity fuck, fuck, fuck!

The uneasy feeling engulfs me as we continue to walk home in silence, albeit with our arms remaining linked around each other's. Physically we look the same as we did two minutes ago, but now our brains are charged – we're both clearly off in our own little worlds and, on my part at least, mulling over what we just said or, rather, didn't say.

'What are you thinking about?' I ask eventually, my voice giving a little squeak.

'I don't know actually . . . I don't think I was thinking about anything,' he says, screwing up his face.

'Really?' I reply, frowning as we walk past a group of drunken teenagers who're loudly arguing over the significance of mistletoe.

I don't buy the notion that not a single thought has passed through Brett's brain since we last spoke. Our minds are never still – there is always something being processed, something being pondered upon . . . How can he not have been thinking about anything?

'You must've been thinking about something,' I grumble, aware that I sound slightly insane and unsure as to what I want him to say.

(Well, no, that's not quite true – I want him to admit to having been thinking about our glittering future.)

'Wait,' he says thoughtfully. 'There was something.'

'Oh?' There's hope . . .

'I was thinking about Christmas Day and whether my nan's going to be making her cranberry sauce.'

'Right.'

'It's just as good as her jam – you'd love it. I'll save you some, though,' he grins, nudging into me.

Well that's enough to put me firmly into a strop. I sulk the rest of the way home, not really engaging with any of the meaningless conversation that Brett comes out with – although he seems to be perfectly happy talking to himself about his Christmas Day ponderings (after the sauce he starts to wonder whether the *Doctor Who* special is going to factor in the death of Clara Oswald or not, and whether his mum would've bought Quality Street or Roses for the Christmas treat table). He doesn't seem to notice that I've clocked out, or that I'm mightily pissed off at him for not recognising in the slightest that I'm pissed off at him.

He remains bright and oblivious all the way home, staying cheerful as we brush our teeth and get ready for bed, then merrily planting a kiss on my lips without even flinching when my lips don't kiss his back.

Even when I roll over and put my back to him (wanting distance between us and trying to hammer home the fact that his attitude has irritated me), he follows and curls his arm around my body – totally blind to tonight's faux pas.

He snores within minutes, leaving me seething into the darkness as I lie under his heavy arm.

I stay awake for hours, working myself up over the significance of Brett's dismissive stance on our future . . . flitting between full-on anger at his indifference and fear of the unknown, and what's to become of us.

4.

I wake up to find Brett sat on top of the covers with his back to me. He is fully clothed and the smell of floral soap fills the air – which means that he's already got up, showered and dressed before even stirring me, which isn't like him. He usually wakes me up the second he catches his first morning breath – or at least seeks out my naked body with a wandering hand.

Something stops me from saying anything to him. Instead, I sit and watch, trying to figure out what he's doing.

Suddenly his shoulders start moving up and down, the force of them causing the whole bed and then bedroom to shake. He's sobbing, I realise with a jolt.

A howl, an earthy, guttural howl, seeps from his mouth and echoes through the cold air around us.

'Why aren't you saying anything?' he croaks, clearly in pain.

'What do you want me to say?' I ask, confused and bewildered at the sight and sound of him being so broken.

'What do you think you should say?' he asks with a hint of bitterness.

'Erm . . .' I panic, feeling as though I'm being tested.

'Quickly.'

'Sorry?'

'Yeah?' he questions.

'Yeah . . .'

'I'm sorry too.'

'For what?' I squeak.

'The end,' he says flatly, with little to no emotion. 'Everything ends.'

'And everything begins,' I say pathetically, not fully grasping what's happening.

The conversation makes absolutely no sense, but as he gets up from the bed he picks up two huge birdcages, as though they're suitcases, and heads towards the door – without even looking back.

I'm hit with a realisation.

He's leaving me.

'Why?' I ask, desperation pouring out of me, willing him to stay.

'Why not?'

'Don't you love me?' I whimper, my face contorting into something ugly.

'Sometimes love isn't enough,' he replies – his voice flat and uncaring.

'Of course it is. Love is all you need . . . All you need is love.'

'Are you quoting Beatles' lyrics?' he frowns, glancing back at me.

'Love me do . . .' I plead.

'Sarah . . .'

'Give me love . . .'

'Stop it,' he demands, shaking his head. 'That was a George Harrison song anyway,' he mumbles to his feet.

'He was a Beatle,' I answer defiantly.

'But he sang it when the band was over.' Pause. 'Apt, I guess . . .'

'We're not over,' I shout, bashing the duvet with my fists.

Brett sighs as he looks at me, the expression on his face one of pity.

It stops my whining, my lashing out, my shouting . . .

I'm still.

'Is there anything I can do to change your mind?' I beg.

His face screws up at the question as he heads out of my bedroom door, towards an awaiting sleigh that's resting on a mound of snow. He slings the birdcages into the back, throws on a red jacket and hat before climbing aboard.

'It would never have worked,' he calls back to me, as he picks up a whip and starts shouting demands at the reindeer in front of him. 'On Sleepy, on Grumpy and Dopey and Doc. On Bashful and Happy and Sneezy – tick tock.'

I sit still on my bed and watch as they charge forward and fly into the dark night's sky, taking with them my one true love – knowing he'll never return.

'Shhhh . . .' he soothes, wrapping his arm around me.

'What?' I mumble, feeling groggy as my head and body come back to reality and away from my dreamland.

'You OK?' Brett asks.

'Yeah . . .' I sniff, wiping my hand across my wet face.

'You were crying.'

'I was?'

'Whimpering like you were in pain.'

'Oh . . .' I say, feeling embarrassed – that was one dream I really don't want to have to voice out loud.

'What was it?' he asks, his face looking just as kind and loving as normal, making my insides soften.

'Oh, just something silly,' I start – stopping myself when I realise what's he's wearing.

'You're in your suit.'

'Of course I am. I'm going to work,' he shrugs.

'But you didn't wake me.'

'I have to go in earlier today.'

'But you always wake me.'

'You looked so comfortable, though – well, until you started getting fretful . . .'

'Yeah,' I say, frowning at the air around me – not liking the fact that this simple little jarring detail from my dream has been echoed in real life.

Brett kisses the top of my head and brings his eyes level with mine, looking at me with concern. 'You feeling better?'

'It was just a dream . . .' I mumble.

'When is it ever just a dream with you?' he asks, flashing a thoughtful smile.

Well, I hope that one was, I think to myself.

'I'd better go,' he sighs, slapping his knees before getting up from the bed.

'Are you here tonight?' I ask, hearing how feeble I sound in my own head.

'I can't,' he says, matter-of-factly. 'It's the work Christmas do.'

'Of course . . .' I sigh, miserably.

'Nothing flashy like last year though – not without you in charge,' he smirks, grabbing his bag from

33

the corner of the room and flinging it over his shoulder.

The previous year I'd worked alongside Brett at Red Brick Productions and was stuck in a thankless job with a feckless boss. The only major upshot was that I got to organise the office party – although that turned out to be a massive con to shield the fact that my boss was having it off with one of the others PAs. There was quite a scene when his wife turned up and caught the pair of them in the cloakroom getting up to no good – or as his wife phrased it 'with his cock in her mouth'. Even though I didn't actually see it (thankfully), the image is still ingrained in my brain somehow – my imagination haunting me with their possible lewd sexual preferences.

Yuck.

'Can't imagine it'll be quite as eventful either,' he muses, with a wink.

'I flipping hope not!' I say, grabbing my pillow and bashing him with it – I don't want to hear of any scandalous behaviour within the company, and I certainly don't want Brett getting tempted by any of my former colleagues (like Poutmouth Louisa who, quite simply, is a giant slut who hates my guts).

'You've nothing to worry about. See you later,' he says, kissing me softly on the lips before placing the pillow beside me and walking out the door.

I'm thankful to find there's not a sleigh, reindeer, or Santa outfit in sight through the open doorway . . .

'You're up,' says Carly, bouncing into my room and

climbing into my bed as we hear the front door closing behind Brett.

'Where's Josh?' I ask.

'In the shower,' she says, biting her top lip as though she's trying to stop a cheeky grin from exploding across her face. She fails, and so buries her happy head under the duvet.

'What?' I ask, tugging at the covers, suspicious of the look she's trying desperately to hide.

'We're going to look at some flats tonight,' she mumbles, her green eyes peeping out over the fabric.

'Woah! What's the rush?' I shriek.

I'm aware of the panic in my voice, but I didn't realise their move was going to be so imminent.

Carly laughs, burrowing her way to me under the covers and giving my waist a cuddle (thankfully I actually slept in knickers and a T-shirt last night and not naked like in my dream). She cuddles into me and rests her head on my shoulder. 'Why wait?' she asks with a sigh.

'I guess . . . You OK?'

'Yeah . . .'

'Sure?' I ask, doing that thing that best friends do where we ask questions without actually having to speak in full sentences. Just letting the other one know that the floor is open to have a certain discussion if they so wish, but that it's OK not to talk about it if they'd rather not.

'I think everything has turned out as it should've done,' she says thoughtfully.

I don't respond, instead letting my silence encourage her, inviting her to share more.

'I still think about what happened every now and then,' she continues. 'I mean, not as much as I used to, obviously – there was a time when I never thought I'd stop thinking about it. But now, from time to time, a thought creeps up on me. I'll be stood watching some parents play with their kids in the park and I'll find myself wondering whether our little creation was a boy or girl, or whether they would've looked like me or Josh . . . Or sometimes, when I'm sat with you guys in the pub, nursing a drink at the end of a hard day at work, I have a split second's thought about how different our lives would be in that moment if things had worked out differently. I'd have a six-month-old baby by now!'

'Not quite so many pub trips then . . .'

'Exactly!' she says, raising her arms to the room as though the thought is ludicrous.

Her dramatics make me laugh, although she quickly shifts back into her reflective mood with her body curled into mine.

'Lexie will be a great mum,' she exclaims. 'Plus, she's married. She won't have to put up with any of the crap I would've done. People didn't even know me and Josh were dating, for fuck's sake.'

'It would've been fine. We're not living in the eighteen hundreds. There are plenty of unmarried couples raising babies.'

'Yeah, I know,' she tuts. 'But there's a reason people

generally go for the more conventional route. Although I was the result of a quick bonk at sea.'

'And you're flipping fabulous!' I wink.

Carly shrugs. 'So, how do you think Dan's going to cope?'

'With the sleepless nights?'

'And the poop-machine ruining all of his designer tops,' she laughs.

'I actually think he'll be a natural . . . as much as it pains me to admit it,' I chuckle to myself. Dan has this quality about him that puts him up there with a Disney character. He's happy-go-lucky and has a real youth about him. Sure, the early days might be a bit hairy (my brother Max likened his first few weeks of fatherhood to relentless torture), but he'll be hands-on and devoted – of that I'm sure.

'My mum seems to think we're all natural parents,' she muses, kicking her feet out from beneath the duvet.

'We should be – it's in our genetics to want to nurture our offspring, I guess.'

'Yeah, but can you imagine Alastair carrying around a changing bag and wearing a top covered in fresh baby sick?'

'Ha! Stranger things, little one, stranger things . . .' I giggle, expecting that even our trendy bestie will make a superb dad when the time comes. 'He might just not be as well kept as he is now.'

'True. What about you?' she asks, moving her head from my shoulder and flipping on to her tummy so that she can see my face. 'How are things going with Brett?'

'Fine.' I shrug, suddenly feeling reluctant to talk about the niggles in my brain.

'And?'

'And?'

'Do you think he'll move in here?' she asks slowly, as though I'm dumb for not knowing what she's referring to.

'I don't know.'

'Why not? It's a great flat – affordable, great location . . .'

'It's not me you have to sell the idea to,' I say forlornly, knowing she's not about to stop her tirade of questions any time soon.

'So you'd be up for it?' she asks, looking at me hopefully.

'If he wanted to, of course.'

'Then what's wrong?'

'I don't know if he wants to,' I admit, unable to hide the bleakness from my voice.

'Don't be an idiot,' she scoffs.

'I'm not.'

'You are.'

'Carly!'

'Why would he not want to live with you? The guy wants to tie you down and knock you up – I'm telling you.'

'Said so romantically,' I laugh, trying my best to hide the doubt stirring inside and hoping beyond hope that my brain and dreams are just conspiring against me to weird me out or confuse me – yes, it's pretty spiteful if that's the case, but it's better than the alternative of them being right and having Brett slip away from me.

'Shower's free,' calls Josh, grinning as he wanders past with a fluffy pink towel wrapped around his waist – a sight I'll be rather thankful to say good-bye to.

'Don't overthink this,' Carly says, giving me a kiss on the cheek, scrambling out of my bed and running towards the door to get into the bathroom before me – even though I've not made a single effort to move from the spot she found me in. 'And don't be a twat,' she warns, stopping to wag her finger at me.

'I'll try my best,' I say honestly, wondering if my best is going to be good enough on this occasion.

5.

Miraculously, I don't dream that night, but, actually, I think that's more because I get hardly any sleep, knowing that Brett isn't by my side and I'm left worrying about what exactly is going on in his head. I mean, I know he's not off with another woman – I trust him– but I'm sure something is going on that I can't quite pinpoint, and that scares me. He's usually so easy to read.

Is it possible that I've just fabricated the whole thing? Let's face it, it wouldn't be the first time my mind has played tricks on me, especially at the helping hands of my nightly unconscious escapades. It's entirely possible that the moment of doubt over my current life fulfilment after the pub quiz led to me feeding that crappy wobble into my dreams – which, in turn, transpired into a nightmare and totally freaked me out, making the whole thing ten times bigger than it actually is. But even if that is the case, I wouldn't be able to blow something up that didn't exist . . . right? There really is no smoke without fire – unless what I'm seeing isn't actually smoke, of course. It could just be a load of misty air vapour that's clouding my vision . . . Oh, who am I trying to kid?!

Needless to say, my frazzled mind spends the

evening tying itself in knots and being completely unhelpful and not buying into any of the things I try to distract myself with: a relaxing bath with super-expensive bubbles (birthday present from Mum and Dad that I haven't used), re-runs of *One Born Every Minute* (I tend to find it utterly terrifying and beautiful at the same time, although on this occasion I fail to shed a tear because I wasn't focusing on it properly) and a giant helping of strawberry cheesecake Häagen-Dazs ice cream (my favourite flavour and I barely managed a quarter of the tub – I'm usually capable of devouring a 500ml portion in a single sitting).

The worst is that I use every ounce of self-control in my possession to stop myself from texting or calling Brett; even when I slip into bed and prepare to go to sleep – which is ridiculous because, on the occasions that we aren't together in the evenings, it's unheard of for us not to speak in some form before we head into the world of dreams.

All my stubbornness brings me is a night of feeling unfulfilled and agitated as I continuously check my phone (which I put on silent to stop myself from replying if he did contact me – an utterly pathetic and stupid idea which leaves me checking it more than ever).

So I toss and turn all night and end up feeling disgruntled and irked when I walk along the canal towards the tube station the following morning.

When I walk past The Barge Café I even feel my

nostrils flare at the memory of our first dream encounter there – I spotted Brett sat sipping on an espresso after being served by Dermot O'Leary.

My body is slumped and heavy, resulting in me feeling like my teenage self. Filled with drama and angst.

Argh.

He didn't call and he didn't text.

How shit.

When I get into the office, I throw my bag on my desk, pick up my red notebook and head straight into an end-of-year meeting with the rest of the team and the bosses.

Surprisingly, the meeting takes us all the way up until lunchtime. When I get back to my discarded bag and am reunited with my phone I'm greeted with two missed calls and two texts from Brett. The first reads:

> Morning, gorgeous. Sorry I didn't text last night. Got in late and didn't want to wake you. Thought you'd value your sleep after the morning's weird dream . . . xx

The second simply reads:

> Hey – you OK? xx

Just as I'm about to write out a light and breezy reply (because I am nothing but light and breezy in this current situation), my phone starts flashing, telling me he's calling again.

'Hello,' I sing – see, light and breezy.

'There you are. I was worried,' he puffs.

'Why?'

'Because you hadn't been in touch . . . ?'

'Oh?' I reply, as though I'm not aware of my silence or the fact that I'm acting like a total bunny boiler just because he didn't instantly say that he wants to watch me grow old and wrinkly.

'What's up?'

'Nothing – just been in a meeting. How was last night?' I ask nonchalantly, as if I'd forgotten all about it.

'All right, I guess.'

'Yeah? No gossip to report?'

'Nope. It was a quiet one really.'

'Nice,' I say, knowing that he's telling the truth – I would never expect anything sordid or disloyal from him. 'Are you OK?' I sigh heavily, feeling foolish as I ask.

'In what way?'

'*Every* way.'

'Cryptic!' He laughs. 'Yes, I think I'm OK in every way.'

'Good.'

'Chinese tonight?'

'Yours or mine?' I ask, relieved that he wants to spend time with me while mentally slapping myself across the face for making myself worry so much – he's being nothing but lovely.

'Yours,' he says quickly. 'Mine's a dump.'

'Really? But you're always so tidy?' I say, hating the suspicious feeling that's still rooting away inside.

'Your Christmas presents are out and unwrapped,' he says, smiling into the phone.

I laugh – what girl doesn't like getting presents? Unless it's some tacky underwear that she wouldn't be caught dead in, of course. Yeah, I find men buying undies creepy and weird. The thought of them stood in shops perving over it all, wondering what they'd like to see their lady in – it's odd. I'd much rather decide that for myself, thank you very much. Although, it's not like it ever stays on for very long anyway, is it? Whipped off within the first few seconds with me.

God, I hope he's not bought me some lacy negligée.

'I'd hide it somewhere, but it won't fit in any of the cupboards,' Brett teases.

'Really?' I say, smiling that the frilly knicker idea has been erased from the equation – well, unless he's bought a mountain of the stuff. 'Fine, you can come to mine,' I gush – surprised that I'm feeling like such a giddy kid over getting a present.

'See you later,' he says.

'Love you.'

'You too.'

I sigh at my phone and nibble on my bottom lip – he really is a dream.

'I spoke to Julian today,' Brett says as we're stood at the kitchen counter serving up our Chinese takeaway from the clear plastic tubs on to our square white china plates.

'Really?' I ask.

Julian is the other love of my life. When I was working at Red Brick Productions with Brett, I came up with a concept for a show called *Grannies Go Gap* – all about getting elderly people out of their comfort zones and showing them that it's not too late to explore the world and make the most of the life they have left. When we were researching and looking for our case studies to pitch the idea to the bosses, we found Julian. In his late seventies, Julian had moved himself into an old people's home when his wife had sadly died. Unsure how else to spend the rest of his days, he figured that at the very least he'd have company on a daily basis. Well, he's such a ball of sunshine that we basically invited him on to the project straight away.

I was gutted that walking out on Red Brick meant that I was leaving Julian and the project behind too, but it was complex and I knew it was in safe hands with Brett at the helm – keeping charge of my baby.

The duo (and a whole production team) scooted off to Australia and New Zealand for a whole six weeks in March. Since then the series has been promoted and aired (to fabulous reviews and has been tipped to bag a National Television Award in a few weeks), with Julian capturing the hearts of the nation. He's not stopped and is currently working on a book deal with Penguin Random House that's seen him take on even more travelling around the globe and documenting his findings. There's no stopping him now he's got the travel bug.

'He's in Thailand at the moment,' Brett tells me.

'Really? Sunning himself on the beach?'

'Actually, doing some volunteer work at an elephant sanctuary.'

'No way!' I laugh, the thought making me feel emotional.

'I know – he's got more excitement in his life than us right now.'

'Our life *is* exciting,' I snap, hastily pouring sweet and sour sauce over my egg-fried rice.

'Of course it is,' Brett smirks, chuckling to himself.

'What?' I sulk, frowning at him.

'We're sat indoors on a Friday night feeling elated over a takeaway and some beers – he's living life on another level, babe.'

'I find this exciting,' I mumble, forking a pork ball into my mouth to shut me up.

With my plate loaded, I wander into the lounge and curl my feet up under myself on the sofa.

'I never said I didn't,' he winks, continuing the conversation as he walks into the room and switches on the TV, falling on to the sofa next to me. 'I'm just saying – we found a really inspirational guy.'

'We did.' I nod in agreement, hating myself for taking everything Brett says to heart like some hormonal teen. 'Just don't pack up and leave me one day to travel the world.'

'As if I would do that!' He laughs.

I munch sadly on my chow mein, hoping he's right.

'You, Nat and Carly are Christmas shopping tomorrow, right?' he asks.

'Yes — although God knows why we're going to Oxford Street and haven't just ordered the lot online. It's going to be chaos.'

'Full of panic buyers,' he nods. 'So glad I'm not joining you.'

'What are you doing?'

'Just seeing some friends.' He shrugs.

'Who?'

'Uni mates,' he says, gulping on his bottle of Tsing-tao. 'Mark, Gary . . . Rob.'

'Right. Well, that will be fun, won't it?'

'I'm dreading it, to be fair.' He frowns, putting the bottle back on the floor by his feet.

'Why?'

'They're not really my sort.'

'Really?'

'We've just grown apart — we're not like you lot.'

'But everyone's your sort,' I say, making him laugh.

'You've got to explain that one,' he says with a cheeky smile.

'I mean, you're friendly and outgoing — you get on with everyone.'

'Ahhh, I love you.' He beams at me, picking up the controls and flicking through the channels. 'What do you fancy watching? *Elf* is about to start.'

'Sold,' I grin, knowing the one thing that's bound

47

to bring me out of my grumpy ways is Buddy singing loud for all to hear. 'Are you staying over tomorrow night after seeing your mates?'

'I was planning on it.'

'Great. Don't forget we have my mum's on Sunday . . .' However, he's zoned out and is occupied with taking his ringing phone out of his pocket instead. He cancels the call and puts it face down on the arm of the sofa, acting blasé as he picks up his fork and spoons a mouthful of food into his gob.

'Who was that?'

'Wrong number,' he muffles, putting his hand over his full mouth to stop rice spraying everywhere as he hastily swallows.

He doesn't look at me, instead his attention turns to Buddy as the tops of his cheeks start to burn slightly red.

He's hiding something.

And now, even worse than that – he knows I know he's hiding something.

6.

I'm sat up high (really, really high), looking down on a bunch of green branches and spikes, all frosted with twinkly lights, metallic shiny rope and huge red balls swinging in the cold breeze that swirls around us.

I'm on a Christmas tree.

Not only that, but, looking down at my clothes (I'm in a cream puffy dress that would've looked great on one of my old Barbie dolls but makes me look like a frumpy lump), I realise I'm the fairy perched up high – sprinkling down her festive magic and overlooking the jolly proceedings, making sure the room is filled with love and happiness. Although, that being said, there's no one else in the room. Just me, a whole heap of presents and a table overloaded with food.

I wait a few minutes to see if anyone is going to enter, but quickly become unable to stop my tummy rumbling because of the gorgeous aroma from the feast below.

Slowly, I unhook myself from the branch behind me and start to clamber down. I've almost made it to the bottom when my stupid fairy skirt gets caught on a bauble hook. I yank at it – ripping the fabric and causing the fragile decoration to ping from its spot and tumble towards the ground. It lands with a crash as shards of glass scatter everywhere.

I wait anxiously, looking to see if the noise is going to alert anyone to the fact that the fairy has absconded from her spot up high.

No one comes.

I jump from the bottom branch and scurry along the floor and up the table leg where I am greeted with the most beautiful sight ever — gigantic food bowls filled with everything a fabulous Christmas dinner requires: turkey (although quite terrifying in its mammoth size), rosemary roast potatoes, brussel sprouts coated with butter and sprinkled with bacon, pigs in blankets (all crisp and mouth-watering), stuffing (the regular Paxo sort — no point ruining a good spread with anything else), fluffy Yorkshire puddings, honey-glazed parsnips and carrots . . . it's all there looking totally scrumptious.

I dive into the potatoes first — munching on their crisp outer skin before whipping out their soft insides . . . I'm in heaven. Best of all, I'm on my own, meaning I don't have that Christmas Day guilt of eating more white potato than is socially acceptable in this day and age, where eating anything white is considered a diet sin.

Bugger that! Orgasmic noises spill from my mouth as I shove more and more in.

I'm about to move on to the juicy-looking pigs in blankets when I hear laughter coming from outside the room.

I freeze. Aware that I'm not going to make it back up to the top of the tree in time, I dive under the table and watch as three pairs of bare feet come wandering into the space.

It's Carly, Natalia and Lexie — all carrying more presents to put under the tree. Sensing I'm not in too much danger, I quietly tiptoe forwards to get a better view while keeping myself out of sight. They may be my best friends — but I'm still a miniature version of myself and I know they'll totally freak out if they see me.

'Oh no, where's the fairy gone?' Natalia asks, looking around the room with confusion. 'Did we forget to put her up there?'

'No – she was definitely there when we left,' says Lexie with a frown.

'Weird,' says Carly. 'She must've fallen down.'

'She's here!' Natalia says as I see her face peering under the table. She grabs my leg and pulls me towards her before lovingly cradling me and brushing off all the fluff, dust and crumbs I've accumulated since leaving my designated spot. 'That's better. Let's put you back where you belong.'

As she walks back towards the tree, I suddenly remember the fallen bauble – the splatter of glass on the floor.

But there's nothing I can do.

'Owwwwwww!' Natalia screams in pain, dropping me to the ground face first.

I'm left in darkness, but I can feel the vibrations of Natalia hopping around on one foot and Carly and Lexie running to help her. I can hear the cries of agony from my wounded friend and the thick drips of blood as they come crashing down on the wooden floor next to me.

The upbeat rhythmic synths of Pharrell's 'Happy' fills the room before the drums kick in along with his velvety voice – filling the room with happiness. I used to wake up to The Killers with *Mr Brightside*, but being in a relationship made me do the ultra giddy thing and change it to this obscenely cheerful and catchy tune.

Usually it sets the tone for the day – I find myself

dancing in the shower, smiling at strangers and even helping tourists with their suitcases on the Tube (rather than just tutting when I'm caught behind them struggling on the stairs).

Today though, the happiness doesn't sit well with the imagery of my dream. Instead, it jars and leaves me feeling uncomfortable.

That's the second dream in only a few days where hastily yanking at a body part or my clothes has resulted in an accident and physical pain. Obviously Natalia getting glass stuck in her foot doesn't quite carry the same horrific sight as all my teeth falling out, but those cries of pain were something else.

I lie there thinking through the possible meaning hidden behind the two events and wonder if there's a life lesson in there – to stop and evaluate a situation when I find myself in a sticky spot, rather than ploughing forward and hoping for the best . . . If I bend and manipulate that enough, I can definitely mould it to fit and give meaning to what is (or isn't) occurring between me and Brett.

Perhaps that's a friendly way of my dreams telling me the same thing Carly warned me about – essentially to make sure I don't become a twat and ruin things. Well, I've certainly been in danger of doing that with my brattish behaviour. Seriously, I haven't even liked myself over the past few days. I don't know how Brett hasn't ducked out and run for cover.

'Hmmm . . .' he croaks, pulling me into him and nuzzling his light morning stubble against my cheek.

Funny, whenever Dan used to grow his beard out I would have a complete hissy fit and threaten to go on a shaving strike myself. Stating that if I had to put up with his rough hair giving me a rash, then he could put up with me looking like a gorilla. Needless to say, he never listened and I never carried through with the threat (I like being smooth), but there's something about Brett's coarse stubble tickling my face that I rather love – perhaps it's because he never rubs it harshly against my face like cheese going through a grater.

'Sleep well?' he asks, his eyes still shut.

'I didn't even hear you come in,' I say, slightly stunned that I slept through a man getting into my bed – albeit my man.

'You must've been knackered from all that shopping.'

'Not so much the shopping but dodging the huge crowds. Seriously, that should be part of the Winter Olympics. It was chaos.'

'I can see it now – elbows at the ready,' he grins, kissing my neck.

'The worst was Hamleys. I only wanted to go in there to get something cuddly for Mavis Rose. I didn't think I'd make it out alive through all the kids and pushy parents barging everywhere. Seriously, I didn't realise being an aunty would be so life-threatening.'

'Hmmm . . .' he groans, giving my neck a deeper kiss and pulling on my hip so that it slides closer into the curve of his body.

'How'd it go with you and your mates?'

'Great,' he shrugs, still on a one-man mission to get a bit of morning action.

'You know we haven't got time for this,' I giggle, wriggling slightly.

'Why not?' he croaks. 'It's a Sunday. This is what we're meant to do on a nice lazy Sunday morning.'

'Except we're going to my mum's and I need time to make myself presentable,' I say with a smile, my body tingling at his touch.

'What are you on about?' he mumbles, nibbling on my earlobe and causing my breath to rise giddily.

'What? My mum's?' I say with a little laugh as I hear him on delay, sure he can't have forgotten our plans.

'Yeah,' he says, suddenly stopping on his quest.

'We're going to my mum and dad's today to have a Christmas get-together because Max and Andrea are spending the actual day with her parents,' I explain, the atmosphere shrivelling up as I twist around to look at him.

'Oh,' he says, looking sheepish.

'You knew that,' I say flatly.

'I didn't realise it was this weekend . . .' he mumbles, frowning as he avoids eye contact with me.

'It's the last Sunday before Christmas, when else were we going to do it?' I ask, starting to get annoyed.

'Sorry.'

'It's not a problem though, is it? You're here, so –'

'Actually –' he starts, cutting me off.

'What?'

'I can't go.' He squirms.

'What the fuck do you mean you can't go?' I shout. I wouldn't normally raise my voice in the flat, but seeing as Carly went and stayed at Josh's last night after our shopping trip I feel free to do so – plus, it's flipping necessary. 'My mum will be furious.'

'I'm sorry, I just can't.'

'Why not?'

'I . . .' He screws his face up as though trying to grab hold of an appropriate answer to give, clearly having difficulty controlling his morning brain. 'I just have somewhere I need to be,' is all he can offer me.

'Well that is just shit!' I yell, throwing the covers off me and storming out of the room to the loo.

Quite simply I need a pee and to defuse my anger away from the situation. By the time I skulk back into the room, Brett is up on his feet and throwing on yesterday's clothes.

'Now what are you doing?' I ask desperately, utterly confused as to how we've got our wires crossed and dreading explaining his absence to my mum.

'Going home.'

'But why?' I whine.

'I told you, I can't go today. I need to be somewhere else.'

'But . . .'

'I'm so sorry. You know I love your crazy mum but I just can't get out of this.'

'You haven't even told me what you're doing.'

'Baby,' he says, coming over to me and grabbing my hand. 'This is totally my fault. I promise I'll make it up to you all.'

'Yeah,' I say miserably, knowing that nothing good can come from me kicking off any further. I'm not his mother and I'm certainly not about to drag him to Kent kicking and screaming against his will so that he can see mine.

'I'll leave now and give you time to get ready.'

'OK,' I mumble, completely defeated.

'Please don't make me feel bad,' he begs.

I sigh into the ground, not wanting to say that I'm fine with him not coming with me, but also not wanting to be a totally unreasonable bitch. If he'd have remembered about today there's no way he'd have made other plans, right?

This is truly just a mistake and miscommunication. It's got to be . . .

'I'll call you later,' he says softly.

'OK.'

'Love you,' he says, cradling my head and planting a kiss on my forehead.

'You too,' I say with a small smile as I watch him leave and feel a heavy weight crash down on me.

'Honestly, I think he's going to dump me,' I find myself saying into my phone half an hour later as I hastily run around the flat getting ready to leave – there's something about going to see my parents that always puts me into a panic. No matter how much time I leave to get my shit together, I'm always scrambling to get myself ready and rushing out the door. In this instance, I'm in even more of a flap because ever since Brett left, my mind has been in overdrive and I've ended up getting myself into a totally anxious tizz.

'Sarah!' Carly groans. 'You promised you wouldn't be a twat.'

'I said I'd try my best.'

'True. I forgot twatdom comes easily to you,' she chuckles.

'Oi,' I squeal, as I sit on the bed and start wrestling with my skinny jeans.

'All right. Tell me why you think the Adonis that is Brett Last is about to call time on your perfectly happy relationship,' she demands. 'You didn't say anything about it yesterday.'

'We couldn't hear each other over the Oxford Street madness,' I explain. It might have been weighing on my mind, but I didn't think shouting out my woes in front of strangers would help to calm my worrying mind.

'True. Go on then. What's he done?' she asks, clearly chewing on her breakfast (I'm guessing a toasted sausage sarnie with ketchup and a light spread of English mustard).

'He's been acting weird,' I state, finally doing up the button on my jeans.

'In what way?'

'I don't know.'

'Yep, you're really on to something there,' she mocks, throwing in a little laugh to let me know she thinks I've totally lost it.

'No, it's hard to pinpoint without sounding absolutely crazy.'

'Maybe you are,' she fires back.

'He's being cagey,' I start, looking at my clothes in my wardrobe and wondering what top to wear.

'Men are,' she replies matter of factly.

'He's been leaving early for work and getting back late.'

'It's Christmas – it's a busy time.'

'He cancelled on coming to see my mum and dad today,' I tut, pulling out a jumper and throwing it over my head.

'Sweetheart, have you just heard yourself? *You'd* cancel on your mum and dad if you could.'

'I know, but . . .' I stammer, knowing that she's right – if there were an option that didn't end with me being left in living hell by not going along, I'd definitely cancel.

'Someone called the other night and he avoided their call and then turned his phone face down on the couch.'

'Could've been a cold caller? Or his mum – I've seen you do the very same thing on multiple occasions to your own mother,' she replies without a hint of concern.

'But it's what people hiding something do!' I moan.

'Is that an actual fact or something you've read about online?' she asks, sounding doubtful over my interpretation of it all.

'He didn't come back here the other night after his work's do.'

'Probably because he doesn't actually live here.'

'But . . .'

'I think this is all in your head,' she says bluntly, stopping me from sounding even more pathetic.

I sigh in frustration. Why do none of these niggles ever sound as big and dramatic as they feel when I voice them out loud?

'You've been dreaming, haven't you?' she asks.

'Noooo . . .' I say, knowing where this part of the conversation is heading – she's going to tell me that it's categorically all in my head and that I'm a total nutcase of a girlfriend.

'You fucking have, you little liar.'

'OK, fine. Yes. Yes, yes, yes – my dreams aren't helping matters,' I sigh, rolling my eyes at the room.

'No wonder you're fuelled with insecurities.'

'But it's more than that,' I moan.

'Sarah Thompson, snap out of it, you big fanny,' she laughs – actually laughs at my woe as though nothing I've told her is in the slightest bit troublesome. 'You've got bigger things to worry about – go make yourself presentable for your mum.'

'God, I don't care what I look like – I've got to explain why my boyfriend hasn't come along to our fake Christmas dinner,' I say, picking up yesterday's socks and giving them a sniff. They're passable for another day's wear. I put them on, then go on a hunt for footwear.

'It'll be fine – but making sure you look good will soften the blow,' suggests Carly.

'Maybe.'

'What are you wearing?'

'Skinny jeans and a snowman jumper.'

'Eeeeeeessssh.'

'What? It's a Christmas gathering – I'm meant to look festive and foolish.'

'Just do your hair and send them my love,' she says before wishing me luck and putting down the phone.

I'll be honest, she's done nothing to lessen my anxiety over my potential impending break-up (and let's face it – you don't piss off the in-laws if you want them on your side forever more . . .), although she has made me feel like a tit now too.

I feel sick as I scroll through the contacts on my phone and call my mum.

'Sarah?' she answers straight away, sounding jolly.

'Morning, Mum,' I say, finding a matching pair of biker boots and quickly sliding them on.

'Have you not left yet? You know what traffic is going to be like this close to Christmas. It'll be rammed if you don't get a move on.'

'Yes, I know, Mum. I'm just about to leave,' I lie, noticing my hair in the mirror and realising there's no way I'd get away with the messy do without a lecture or ribbing comment. It used to be that Mum continuously criticised me over my appearance and job choice because she wanted me to bag a man. Now, however, that's increased ten-fold as she has one single focus and that's to get Brett to make an honest woman of me (whatever that means – because, as far as I'm aware, there's no wiping my colourful slate of a past clean).

God, she's going to be devastated when he dumps me, I realise.

'So why are you calling?' she asks, sounding confused.

'I just thought I'd give you some warning – Brett's not coming with me,' I say, screwing up my face and waiting for the ear bashing that's undoubtedly to follow.

'He's not,' she states.

'Nope.'

'No, I mean, I know he's not.'

'You do?'

'Yes, he's just phoned.'

'Oh?'

'Yes.'

'Well, I'm sorry he's had to cancel,' I say, surprised to hear Brett's gone out of his way to soften Mum's attitude towards me. Perhaps I'm being a bit hard on him.

'Not to worry, I haven't even started cooking yet,' she says, as though she's shrugging and totally unperturbed by the change of plans (not at all like my controlling mother). 'Such a nice man. Honestly,

7.

On the drive to Mum's, I find myself stewing over the morning's events, feeling like my head has swung back to worrying over the future of my relationship and whether Brett is trying to find an easy way out without hurting me. It's unlike him to be scatty and change plans last minute, especially when it's something important like lunch with my family so, deep down, I know I'm not making something out of nothing, despite what Carly says.

'Look at you!' My mum beams at me as soon as I open the door of my car. They usually buzz me in the gates and then wait for me to scramble my stuff together and knock on the front door before they even acknowledge my existence – never am I greeted at the side of my car like they're about to offer some superbly efficient posh valet service.

'Hi, Mum,' I say, awkwardly side-stepping out of my Mini while dragging across my handbag from the passenger seat.

I've barely even stood up straight before my mum has engulfed me into a hug. Now, in any other household a hug from your own mother is normal and nothing new, however, my mum does not hug. Not like this. Not with ... . what even is this?

Love?

Weird.

'You OK? Everything OK with Dad?' I ask, suddenly panicked that one of them has been diagnosed with a terminal illness – that's the only explanation I can muster for such an outpouring of affection.

'All good. Your dad's just pruning the plants out back.'

'Aren't they all dead already?' I ask, escaping her grasp and making my way to the boot to collect the sack-load of presents I have for everyone (mostly Mavis Rose).

'They will be soon, but your dad's discovered all sorts of tricks to keep them alive longer. Clever man.'

'Great,' I say, still terrified that she's about to announce that she's seriously ill – she's never this nice to any of us. 'Max not here yet?'

'Going to be late.'

'Oh?'

'I know – one child of their own and they're late to everything. Honestly, I made sure we were never late to a single event when you two were younger. His time-keeping is abysmal.'

I smile. That's more like it. She's clearly not at death's door. 'Can't be helped.'

'Yes,' she sighs. 'Well, come on in, I'll make you some tea. You still drinking peppermint? I've got these new teabags I saw in Waitrose – thought you might like them.'

'Thanks, Mum,' I smile, enjoying the fact that she's gone to that little extra effort for me.

'Such a shame Brett couldn't make it,' she says as she makes her way through the front door of my childhood home and towards the kitchen. 'He sounded awfully apologetic when he called. Bless him. You'll have to take some turkey back with you so you can make sandwiches this week – and some mince pies.'

'There she is,' sings Dad as he comes through from the garden with grass stains on his trousers, waving a pair of shears in the air. He puts them down on the counter and hugs me.

I feel myself sighing as the familiar musky smell of his aftershave wafts up my nostrils, instantly comforting me.

'What have I told you about putting those dirty tools down in here when I'm about to cook!' Mum gasps.

'Sorry, dear,' he apologises, pulling a cheeky face in my direction.

'Now go get out of your gardening clothes – we have guests,' Mum orders, shooing him out of the kitchen while picking up his shears and placing them outside the back door.

'Guests?' I laugh. 'Since when?'

'It's only Sarah,' Dad agrees, on his way to change, shaking his head at her lunacy.

'Just make an effort, dear,' she demands, opening the oven and letting the mouth-watering smell of roasting turkey escape.

The gate buzzer blasts through the house, declaring the arrival of Max, Andrea and Mavis Rose.

'I'll go,' I say, pushing the button on the intercom and heading for the front door, eager to get a glimpse of my niece as they drive in.

It's scary how much Mavis Rose has changed over the last year. I try to see her once every two weeks (at least), and each time it's as though she's learnt to do something new or has a deeper understanding of life. Seriously, sometimes she has such a thoughtful and pondering expression on her face that I'm sure she has a greater grasp of what we're doing on this planet than I do.

'Oh my gosh, look at you,' I say, opening the door and spotting the Christmas Pudding outfit that they've cruelly dressed her in for our amusement.

'Don't you look scrummy,' I add, unlocking her seatbelt clasp and pulling her out.

'Give Aunty Sarah a kiss,' Max calls, climbing out of the car and walking round to us.

'She doesn't do that!' I gasp, looking at her sleepy little cherub face.

'She does,' smiles Andrea, getting out of the passenger side of their huge child-carrier of a car and giving me a hug. 'She might just need warming up first. Are you going to give Aunty Sarah a kiss hello?' she asks Mavis Rose softly – her voice an octave higher than normal.

I pucker up my lips to give her some encouragement.

66

Mavis Rose looks from my eyes to my mouth, her face full of a complex expression, clearly summing me up. She knows she's seen me before – she knows I've made her cackle with laughter and no doubt recalls that I'm the best aunty in the whole wide world ever (actual fact).

I'm about to give up and say I'll try again later, however it seems ten seconds is all the little beauty needs. She leans her head towards me and places her lips on mine. Granted she doesn't pucker up, but it doesn't matter. It was a kiss. The intention was there.

My heart melts.

'Oh my gosh, I could eat you,' I squeal, squeezing her tiny frame into mine.

'Where's Brett?' Max asks, closing the boot of the car after collecting a small bag of presents – let's face it, gifts are never going to be the same again now that we have a little princess to spoil.

'Something came up,' I say, pursing my lips, hating the fact that I can't expand on this further.

'Oh?' he asks, sending a little frown in Andrea's direction, which I wish I hadn't witnessed.

'Never mind. Sure we'll see him soon,' Andrea says, putting her hand around my waist and kissing Mavis Rose on the cheek.

Oh my god.

They think he's going to ditch me too.

Fuck!

*

If it weren't for the utterly delightful Mavis Rose, I'd have spent the entire afternoon drowning in my misery and grunting at everyone. But her laughter and enthusiastic animal noises are enough to keep a smile plastered on my face and a lightness in my heart.

Although, one thing that does cause me to almost wobble from my semi-stable state of avoidance is my mother, who spends the entire five hours I'm in her company continuing to be uncharacteristically nice to me. It's a total mind-fuck.

Where have the sarcastic comments and digs about my appearance disappeared to? I mean, I'm aware that my hair looks a total mess (it only gets worse once Mavis Rose has had a few yanks of it), but she doesn't mention it once. Not once! What's got into her?

Seriously, I don't know what she's playing at, but my mum being nothing but charming is enough to totally freak me out. I'm relieved when I get back in my car (with a box filled with treats for Brett) and head back to the flat.

8.

The following days zoom by (thankfully), due to us having to tie up deals before Christmas and having to have merry schmoozes with our contacts at various channels to keep them on board. Before I know it, it's Wednesday and my last day at work. Kindly we've been given Christmas Eve off (everywhere in production is slowly becoming dead and unresponsive so it makes no sense to be in the office when the rest of the industry have left for the holidays), and we're even allowed to slink off at midday to 'get ourselves ready for the festive days ahead of us'. How flipping lovely.

That being said, Brett still has to work – it's not like Red Brick Productions to treat their staff to an extra day paid holiday just for the hell of it, so I spend the afternoon on my own in the flat, wrapping up Christmas presents, soaking in the bath and wondering how and when Brett is going to finish with me. With Christmas only a day and a half away, he'd be pretty cold to do it now but, likewise, breaking someone's heart at this time of year when they're with family, friends and have time free to stuff their faces with food and wine is possibly the kindest thing someone can offer you when they've ripped your heart out and discarded you back on to the shelf of doom.

Sarah – I don't know how you managed it. See you soon,' she says, putting down the phone.

Well, that was a backhanded compliment if ever I heard one . . . Deciding to stick with my messy ponytail, I grab hold of my Mulberry bag (I treated myself to a steel-blue Bayswater as an early Christmas present), chuck in my essentials, snatch up my car keys and get ready for an afternoon in the countryside.

'You ready?' Carly shouts from her room as I'm throwing on a new festive jumper – I'm a Christmas tree complete with knitted baubles and tinsel. I was in two minds whether to wear it after my dream, but it's not as though I'm going to be able to avoid the bloody things, is it? Might as well embrace the mayhem.

'Yep, ready,' I reply as she walks into my room wearing an even more ridiculous piece of knitwear – one of Rudolf the Red Nose Reindeer, complete with a shiny and bulbous red nose and antlers sticking up from her shoulders. 'How on earth are you going to wear a coat?' I ask, unable to stifle a laugh.

'I'll find a way,' she shrugs, picking one up and jabbing an arm inside.

Our comical jumpers have become a tradition for the final pub quiz of the year. We all try and get our hands on the most stupid and wacky concoctions we can find and goofily wear them together – united with our silliness. Although I'm pretty sure the boys wait until they're round the corner before donning them . . . not that I mind. Us girls just seem more at peace with making tits of ourselves. Perhaps because it comes so easily to us . . .

The gang have already gathered in their Christmas jumper frenzy when we arrive and have got in the first round of drinks, along with crisps, nuts, pork scratchings and Scampi Fries – whoever ordered it all has seriously indulged in the snackage. Especially as we'll be munching on a Christmas dinner a bit later too – still, this'll tide us over and stop us getting cranky. We all love each other, but even we can't avoid hunger moodiness if we're not regularly fed.

Looking around the room, I spot that the High-kick-flyers have also assembled. They too have decided to dress up, although they're all dressed to match as Santa's elves with green blazers and matching skirts or shorts, green pointy hats, stripy red and white tights and knee-high green boots. Although I hate to admit it, they actually look really good.

'Where's Brett?' asks Carly, looking around the room.

'Dunno,' I answer. 'He should be here by now though.'

'He's just out back getting ready,' grins Josh.

'Ready?' asks Carly.

'You'll see.'

'Sit down and have a drink,' says Natalia, tugging on my arm so that I land on the chair next to her.

I happily oblige.

'Have you guys been swotting?' asks Alastair from across the table.

'It's all we've thought about.' I nod, my face serious.

'We've done nothing but read up on current affairs all week,' chimes in Carly, also managing to keep a straight face.

'Good, good,' says Dan. 'Lexie's got serious baby brain, so I highly doubt we can count on her for a right answer.'

'Don't be so mean!' Natalia tuts.

'It's true,' Lexie laughs, shrugging off Dan's comment. 'I spent an hour looking for the car keys the other day, only to find I'd put them in the fridge the night before.'

We laugh at her confession.

'I do stuff like that and I don't even have an excuse,' admits Carly.

'She's not joking,' adds Josh.

'Well, I think I'm starting to drive Dan a bit mad,' says Lexie, pulling a worried face at us girls.

'Only when you start a conversation and then completely forget what you were talking about – mid sentence,' he says, looking at all of us for sympathy, or at least for us to acknowledge the chaos he's living in.

'Sounds awful,' says Alastair non-committally as he opens up a fresh bag of scratching and dives into the salty goodness. I say goodness, they're invariably filled with crap and salt – but they just taste so yummy.

'Josh,' calls Becky from the bar. I look up to see her gesturing towards the quizmaster's set-up – a small raised area between the gents' and ladies' loos, on top of which is a desk, a microphone and a speaker. Actually, it's been revamped slightly for the occasion and has fairy lights wound around anything and everything (mic stand, table legs – even flopping over the toilet doors) and the chair has been swapped for a big red throne.

I watch as Josh leaps from his chair and heads over to the microphone.

'Ladies and gentleman, I think we'll all agree that

tonight is the most important night of the calendar year,' he says to a raucous amount of cheers from the different groups in the pub. 'Well, this year, because we've all been extra special good, we have an extra special quizmaster. Would you all please be upstanding and give a warm welcome to . . . Santa!'

A loud laugh flies from my mouth when I spot Brett strutting out from behind the bar in his Santa get-up, carrying a sack of treats. He grins as he high-fives the whole of our group and, strangely enough, my heart flutters when he winks at me before turning to make his way to his lavish seat. Thankfully the sight of him in a Santa costume in my dream hasn't mentally scarred me.

'Thanks for the warm welcome,' he laughs into the mic. 'Phew, it's hot in here,' he says, pulling on his jacket and making us all laugh.

'Get on with it,' shouts out someone from the back.

'Who said that?' asks Brett, squinting around the room. 'Any more backchat and I'll put you on the naughty list, got that?'

The room is silent, like an obedient group of puppies, eager for more.

'Let's start. Everyone got their paper and pens?' he asks, glancing up at the room over the top of the thinly framed gold spectacles he's wearing.

'Wonderful.' He looks down at the paper in front of him and coughs slightly, taking a deep breath before starting. Despite his friendly and jolly manner, I'm sure he must feel nervous at having a room full of people staring at him. I don't know how Ian stands up there every week and leads us all, especially as he isn't overly confident anyway.

'Question one,' he begins. 'Let's start with an easy one. The song "White Christmas"was performed by Bing Crosby in which 1954 film?'

'Easy,' Josh mutters as Alastair picks up the pen to write down *White Christmas* on our sheet of paper without even waiting to confer.

'Are you sure?' asks Dan, who loves to triple-check everything written down each week.

'Positive,' says Alastair, not even considering the fact that he could be wrong.

'Didn't we get tripped up on a similar question last year?' asks Lexie, frowning at Dan.

'That was about the first film the song appeared in – which wasn't *White Christmas*,' explains Alastair.

'Oh.' Lexie nods, shrugging at me, Natalia and Carly.

'Question two: Can you name the original eight reindeer from the "Twas the night Before Christmas" poem?'

Us girls smile as we whisper in unison, 'Now Dasher! Now Dancer! Now Prancer and Vixen! On Comet! On Cupid, on Donner and Blitzen.'

'Did you get that?' grins Josh.

'Yep,' nods Alastair, quickly scribbling on the page in front of him.

'Ho, ho, ho – time for question three,' sings Brett, clearly getting into his character. 'What was Mr Bean searching for when he got his head stuck in a turkey?'

The thought alone is enough to make us smile.

'His watch,' I whisper, just in case the others weren't thinking the same.

'Got it,' nods Alastair.

'And on to question four!' says Brett when a few seconds have passed and the floor of the pub all have their eyes concentrated on him again. 'In the film *Jingle All The Way* what toy was Arnold Schwarzenegger hunting down?'

'Turbo Man,' says Dan with a smirk. 'I so wanted one of those,' he says with a sad shake of his head. 'Never got one.'

'Tragic,' I say, sounding slightly less sympathetic than I mean it to.

'Next question – number five,' says Brett. 'In the *Friends* episode, "The One With Phoebe's Dad", what do Chandler and Joey buy Phoebe?'

'Toilet seat covers,' whispers Natalia with excitement, giving a fabulous Phoebe impression.

The boys write down the answer without even questioning it.

'We're smashing this,' I exclaim, getting giddy at our input as we speed through the next few questions with continued ease – absolutely certain we're answering them correctly.

'Question nine: Which former *I'm a Celeb* female appeared in the 2014 Christmas special of *Come Dine With Me* and took selfies with her food?'

'Argh,' I groan. 'Helen Flanagan.'

'I like her,' says Lexie. 'I think she's totally misunderstood.'

'I don't mind her either,' grins Alastair, cupping his hands in front of his chest as though grabbing hold of a giant pair of melons.

'Gross,' I say, shaking my head at him.

'I'll take that.' He shrugs and picks up the pen, writing down our answer.

'Question ten: Who won the 2014 series of *The X Factor*?'

We all stare at each other open-mouthed.

'You should know this,' says Carly, elbowing me in the ribs. 'You voted for him enough times.'

'Oh fuck . . . ' I grumble, my mind sieving through a sea of faces in my brain. Suddenly the guy in question springs into my mind. 'I have a face!' I exclaim.

'A name, we need a name!' encourages Dan.

'I'm thinking, I'm thinking, I'm thinking, I'm thinking. Ben!' I say, clenching my fists. 'Ben Haenow.'

'Oh, he was fit,' remarks Natalia, giving an approving nod of the head.

'You girls will vote for any half-decent-looking bloke,' says Josh, shaking his head.

'Actually, he was very sweet, too,' I say pathetically, knowing it was his smouldering eyes that caused me to pick up the phone rather than anything else – but at least he could hold a tune. In past years I've simple voted for a pretty face, even if they couldn't hold a note. Sad, but true.

'Is everyone else finding this as easy as us?' I ask, looking around the room.

'Not sure,' says Natalia. 'I've spied the theatre luvvies huffing and puffing – but then, they're only easy questions if you know the answers.'

'And that we do,' I grin.

'So far!' warns Alastair. 'Don't jinx us.'

'Eek!' I squeak.

There's a pause from our very own Santa as he picks up a new pile of question cards and flicks through them, as though checking they're in the correct order. I watch as he licks his lips and takes a gulp of his beer, gripping hold of the glass for a few seconds when it's back down on the table before continuing.

'Right,' he breathes, licking his lips again. 'The next round of five questions are themed around tonight's specialist subject.'

'Merry fucking Christmas!' shouts the same voice as earlier.

'He's warned you!' shouts Josh, much to our astonishment. Josh is our cuddly bear; it's not like him to speak up in this manner.

Brett, nonetheless, is unperturbed. 'Tonight's specialist subject is a rather unique one . . . It's Sarah Thompson,' he says into the mic, grinning over at me as he says it.

'What?' I laugh, as my friends look between the two of us, equally as confused. All, that is, apart from Josh, who's sat with a smug look on his face, clearly aware that this was about to happen.

'What's going on?' Carly whispers loudly at him.

He shrugs as though he has no idea – although his facial expression suggests otherwise.

'Question one of our specialist subject,' Brett says, chuckling to himself, rightly finding the whole thing hilarious.

Seriously, what on earth is he up to?

'In a school report from when she was five years old, teacher Mrs Bottomless said Sarah would be a star pupil if she . . . what?'

I laugh out loud.

'Any idea?' smirks Josh.

'Yes,' I say, raising my eyebrows at him. 'If I didn't spend so much time staring out the window day-dreaming.'

'Sounds about right,' giggles Carly.

Rather than grumble and moan at the interruption to normal pub quiz protocol, the rest of the room seem to actually be getting involved and debating what the answer could be. Which is slightly bizarre as they all turn and glance at me as they talk amongst themselves.

'Question two,' says Brett, pulling his bottom lip through his teeth as he waits for the room to quiet down.

'If asked, Sarah would say that 'Without Love' is her favourite Tom Jones song – but what is it really?'

'He can't actually know the answer to this one,' I half laugh.

'I think this guy knows you pretty well,' smiles Natalia.

'It's got to be one of his cheesy ones, otherwise you'd admit to it anyway,' prompts Dan.

'It is. It's flipping 'Sex Bomb' – but only because I love singing and dancing to it in the shower.'

'Bingo,' says Alastair, taking pen to paper.

'Question three, when he was just five years old, what did Sarah tell her brother Max?' asks Brett with a laugh.

'Oh my god,' I moan, covering up my face with embarrassment.

'What did you do?' squeals Lexie, clapping her hands in excitement.

'I told him he was adopted.'

'Oh, we've all done that,' says Dan.

'Yes, but then I managed to convince him to pack a small suitcase and leave to find his real parents.'

'What?' laughs Carly – half impressed, half disgusted.

'He only got as far as the front door,' I state.

'What stopped him?' asks Josh, seeming to enjoy my squirming.

'Mum heard him dragging his suitcase down the stairs and came to see what all the noise was. I was grounded for a week and had my Barbie dolls taken away for even longer,' I sulk.

'I'm not sure who I feel more sorry for,' says Natalia, looking genuinely mortified by the whole thing.

'Question four – we're almost there, ladies and gentleman,' says Brett, seeming to be enjoying himself, but still looking anxious as hell. 'On a night out

79

at university, Sarah said she witnessed a stranger being sick in her friend Natalia's designer handbag . . . but what actually happened?'

'No!' I gasp, looking at Natalia with my hand over my mouth.

'And, for the record, I was there,' Brett cheekily says into the microphone. 'I saw the events unfold.'

'It was you!' whispers Natalia, her eyes wide in shock.

'I'm *so* sorry,' I groan, putting my arms around her.

Carly cackles crazily beside me – I give her a quick kick under the table but miss.

'You're gross,' says Alastair, shaking his head as he writes down the answer. 'I don't know how we're friends.'

'We should faze her out!' nods Carly in a mocking manner, unable to keep a straight face.

'You guys are just as bad as me,' I say, pointing my finger around the table.

'Even worse,' shrugs Dan, sticking up for me.

'Sounds like everyone's doing well here,' says Brett, taking a deep breath. 'So now onto the final question of this specialist round.'

He stands from his throne of a chair, takes off his Santa hat and, taking the microphone with him, steps off his stage and on to the pub floor.

Ignoring the audible intake of breath from the rest of the pub, he looks only in my direction as he slowly starts walking towards me.

'Sarah Thompson, you are totally bonkers,' he

states with a proud grin that causes my insides to flip and my eyes to go all blurry from the tears that are welling up. 'You watch all sorts of crap on TV, your cooking is questionable, your language is despicable. You have the most vivid imagination of anyone I know when you're awake, but it seems when you're asleep things increase ten-fold. You have the most bizarre, crazy, out-of-this-world dreams – and I know you hide the really insane stuff from me.'

'You bet,' shouts Carly, giggling out loud, causing the rest of the room to laugh along with her.

For a second or two, Brett and I just look at each other as a feeling passes between us that I've never experienced before. I'm full of an emotion bigger than any I've ever felt – a mash up of hope, under-standing, commitment, loyalty, security, but, most of all, an all-consuming and forever-promising love.

Brett smiles at me.

'Since we re-met last year, I've felt like we've been in our own little dream,' he says, licking his lips. 'And I don't ever want to wake up and find that I have to spend a single day without you.'

Stood in front of me, Brett takes out a small blue box from the pocket of his Santa trousers and kneels on the ground. Lifting the lid of the box, I see the sparkle of a diamond ring.

My heart sings.

'Sarah Thompson, I love you. I have done for a long time. Will you do me the honour of becoming Mrs Last? Will you be my wife?'

The suspense in the room as I look from Brett to the ring is indescribable.

I feel as though I'm literally floating above the whole thing as I take in the delighted and shocked (aside from Josh's) faces of my friends and even suddenly spot all of my family at the bar: Mum, Dad, Max, Andrea and Mavis Rose – all grinning widely. They must have been waiting in the back.

I look back at Brett, savouring the beautifully unexpected moment. 'I thought you were going to dump me,' I cry, elation flooding through me. 'Of course I'll marry you! Of course I'll be your wife.'

The ring gets slipped on my finger and, with a slightly forceful push (from my part), goes on perfectly. Brett leaps to his feet and scoops me into his arms, hugging me tightly as our bodies shake with an emotional overload of happiness.

The room erupts into cheers, wolf-whistles and audible sobbing (mostly from Natalia, Carly and a hormonal Lexie), but before anyone can move from the spot they're in, music swells in the room. I look up to see the High-kick-flyers performing an a capella rendition of Mama Cass's 'Dream a Little Dream'.

Complete with 'Oohs', 'Aahs', some practised movement (twirls and swaying, as well as high kicks) and some gentle jingle bell ringing (well, it is Christmas), the song is sung beautifully – much to the delight of my friends who can't help but grin at the absurdness of it all.

'Santa's little helpers,' I muse with a laugh, realising they've even come dressed the part.

'They've taken their role very seriously,' Brett nods sternly before his face cracks into a smile.

As the song continues, landlord Ian and Becky come out from hiding behind the bar with trays laden with glasses filled with celebratory bubbles.

'Totally in on it,' mumbles Brett into my ear when he spots me looking.

'I knew you'd been acting weird,' I say, shaking my head.

'I couldn't help it. You're a hard girl to keep things from – I had the jewellers calling me about picking up the ring one night, I had my Santa costume to collect one morning before work – which, by the way, has been hanging up in my flat for the last few days,' he says, shaking his head as though the whole thing has been chaos.

'So that's why I couldn't come over,' I say, as the events of the last week start to piece together.

'Exactly. Are you aware how difficult it is to hire one of these bad boys in December?' he says, as though the high demand is unusual for this time of year. 'And this is what you were doing on Sunday when you couldn't come to my parents?' I ask, feeling relieved.

'Yes, they already knew what was happening so they understood that I needed time to prepare.'

'No wonder Mum was so nice to me,' I laugh as I spot her sipping on her drink at the bar, tapping her foot to the musical number.

'You must've been so worried.'

'I was!'

'Well, Sunday was tough. It wasn't easy writing a quiz that I was sure you'd know all the answers to.'

'You mean, that was all fixed?' I squeak, pouting my lips to show my utter disappointment. 'I thought I was on a roll.'

'Oh, baby,' he laughs, pulling my head into his chest.

'Well that sucks,' I joke, finding it pretty hard to feel sad about anything right now.

'I was also with Josh picking up the ring and getting this lot sorted out with their involvement on Saturday when you were with the girls,' he says, nodding towards the all-singing, all-dancing troupe in front of us.

'But I thought you were with your friends,' I say, astounded that my mind veered towards thinking I was getting dumped rather than having some flipping amazing frosting added to my wedding finger.

'Mark, Gary and Rob?' Brett laughs mischievously, his arms gripping me tightly around the waist. 'That's only two members away from another Take That reunion.'

'What?'

'Totally fabricated.'

'And you completely avoided my chat about the future!' I say, remembering how I first became completely bummed out when I approached the subject the week before.

'Because I already had this planned and didn't want to spoil it. I thought about just doing it on the spot that night, that's why it took me a second or two to reply,' he laughs. 'I'm so glad I didn't.'

'I've been going crazy wondering what's been up with you,' I sigh, playing with his red faux velvet jacket.

'I know you have and I'm so sorry. I didn't know how I could keep you happy, keep the secret a secret and still get everything done. But you know now and I promise there's going to be no more secrets.'

'You sure about that?'

'Absolutely. I'm madly in love with you,' he whispers, giving me a kiss on the lips before looking into my eyes. 'I want the whole shebang – marriage, the two point four kids, the growing old and wrinkly . . . everything. As long as it's with you.'

'I can't fucking wait,' I giggle, putting my hands on his cheeks and pulling his lips towards mine as the song comes to an end and the room breaks into another round of applause and cheers.

MERRY CHRISTMAS!

'Warm and romantic, this charming read will
certainly brighten up your day' *Closer*

Billy and Me

'A gorgeous, gloriously romantic read with
buckets of charm – I absolutely loved it!'
Jill Mansell

Giovanna Fletcher

The gorgeously romantic story of one small-town
girl and the world's most famous movie star . . .

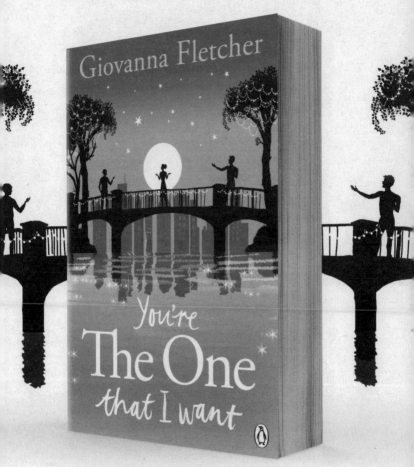

'A heartbreakingly beautiful story about friendship and unrequited love. I was totally and utterly captivated' Paige Toon

Giovanna Fletcher

You're The One that I want

It's Maddy's wedding day but has she made the right choice between the groom and his best man . . . ?

'Saucy, fun and full of heart. This is Giovanna's most accomplished novel yet! This book ticked every one of our must have boxes' *Heat*

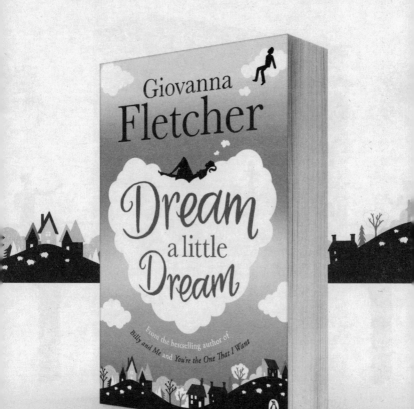

Giovanna Fletcher

Dream a little **Dream**

From the bestselling author of *Billy and Me* and *You're the One That I Want*

Because no one ever really finds the person of their dreams . . . do they?